Arnie was excited when he got a skateboard
for his birthday. It was hard to ride at first.

But before long,
Arnie could go
down the sidewalk and
even turn a little.

ARNIE

and the
Skateboard Gang

NANCY CARLSON

PUFFIN BOOKS

PUFFIN BOOKS

Published by the Penguin Group

Penguin Books USA Inc., 375 Hudson Street, New York, New York 10014, U.S.A.

Penguin Books Ltd, 27 Wrights Lane, London W8 5TZ, England

Penguin Books Australia Ltd, Ringwood, Victoria, Australia

Penguin Books Canada Ltd, 10 Alcorn Avenue, Toronto, Ontario, Canada M4V 3B2

Penguin Books (N.Z.) Ltd, 182-190 Wairau Road, Auckland 10, New Zealand

Penguin Books Ltd, Registered Offices: Harmondsworth, Middlesex, England

First published in the United States of America by Viking,
a division of Penguin Books USA Inc., 1995
Published in Puffin Books, 1997

1 3 5 7 9 10 8 6 4 2

THE LIBRARY OF CONGRESS HAS CATALOGED THE VIKING EDITION AS FOLLOWS:

Carlson, Nancy L.
Arnie and the skateboard gang / Nancy Carlson. p. cm.
Summary: When Arnie is challenged to skateboard down a dangerous hill,
he has to decide how far he is willing to go to be "cool."
ISBN 0-670-85722-X
[1. Skateboarding—Fiction. 2. Courage—Fiction.]
I. Title.
PZ7.C21665Aph 1995   [Fic]—dc20   94-39232   CIP   AC

Puffin Books ISBN 0-14-055840-3

Printed in the United States of America

One day when Arnie was skateboarding, Tina came by. "Hey Arnie,
let's go down to the park. That's
where all the cool skateboarders
hang out," said Tina.

When Tina and Arnie got to the park,

they saw cool kids skateboarding all over.

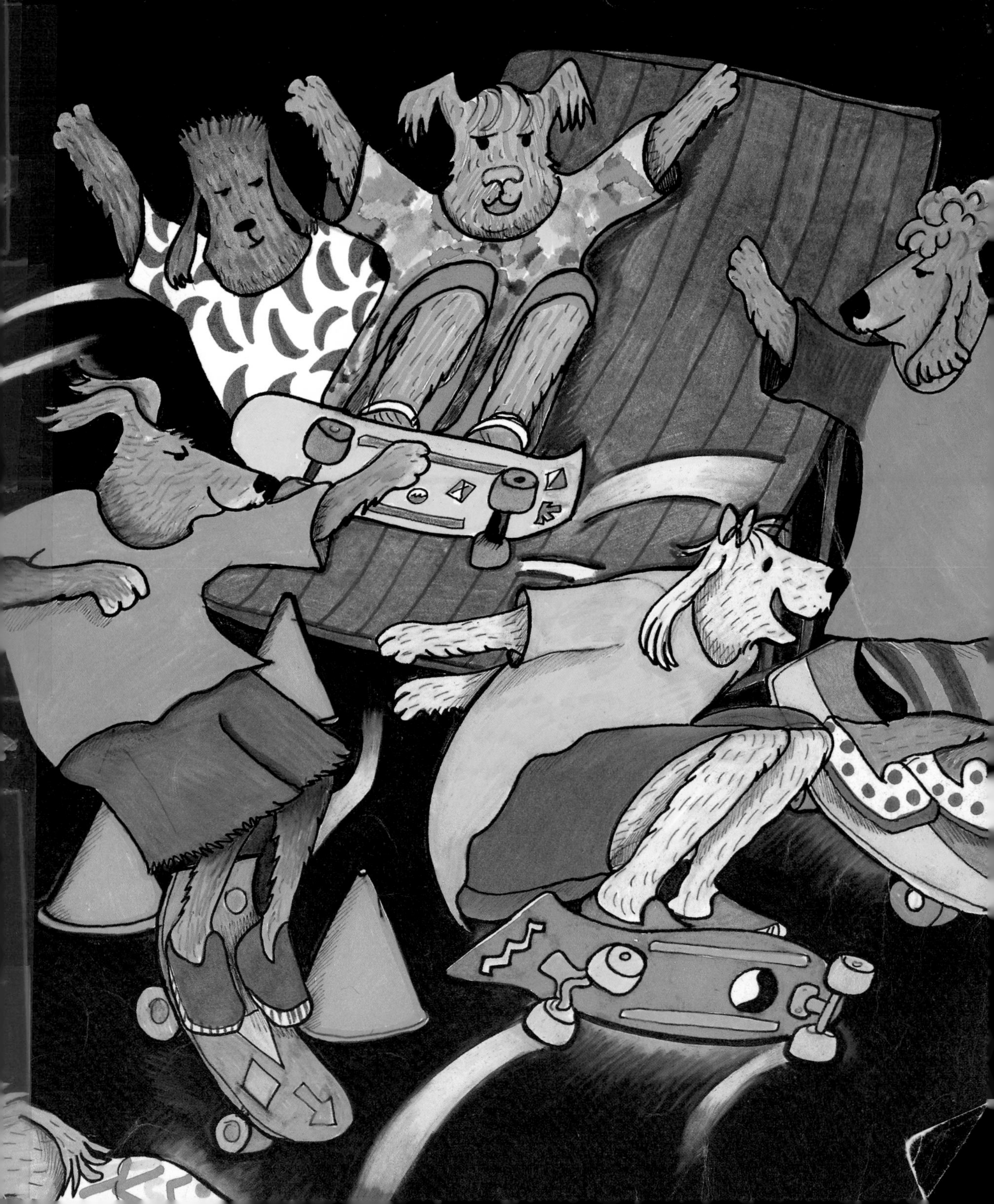

"Awesome!"
said Arnie, as he
watched a kid jump a barrel.

"They call him the Fly," whispered Tina.

"Let's see what you two can do," said the Fly.

Tina tried the ramp. She wiped out!

Arnie tried the jump. He banged his elbow

"You two need lots of practice," laughed the Fly.

"I want to be just like those guys," thought Arnie.

Arnie and Tina
began hanging out

at the park every day
to skateboard.

After lots of practice, Arnie could do the ramp,

and Tina could do the slalom course.

When the Fly saw them he said,
"You two are getting pretty good."

It wasn't long before Arnie and Tina became
regular members of the skateboard gang.

One day when Arnie got to the park, everyone was leaving. "We're going over to Hairy Kerry Hill," said Tina.

"It's going to be cool. You get to go over fifty miles an hour," said the Fly.

When they got to Hairy Kerry Hill,
Arnie could not believe his eyes.

"Who's going first?" asked the Fly

"Okay, okay, I'll go," he said.

The Fly was doing great—until he hit a bump!

"Ouch! Boy, that was one wild ride,"
said the Fly. "Now, who's next?"

When nobody answered, the Fly said,
"You go now Arnie!"

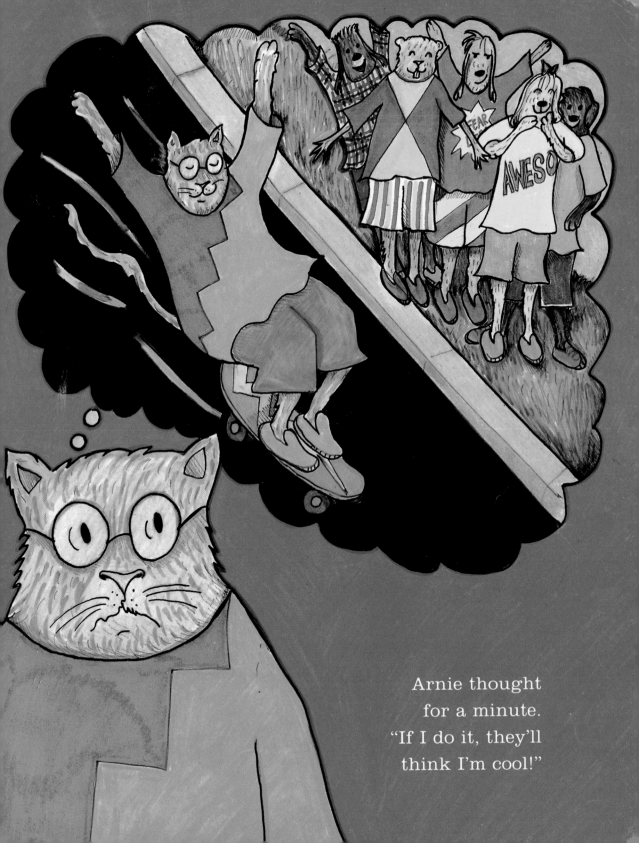

Arnie thought
for a minute.
"If I do it, they'll
think I'm cool!"

"Are you going down
or not?" asked the Fly.

"Are you nuts?" said Arnie. "I'm not going down
that hill. Anyone want to go back to the park?"

"I do!" yelled Tina.

"Let's go!" yelled the gang.

"Hey, wait for me!"
yelled the Fly.